THE CONSTRUCTION WORKER

WRITTEN BY

TOM NORTH

Chapter 1

My feet were bloody killing me. Six o'clock in the morning and my mouth was as dry as Ghandi's flip flop. I'd just about managed to drag myself out of bed and was just slumping along the pavement hovering my hands over my head to shelter from the rain. Just my luck to turn up soaked for the first day.

My mate Ben had managed to get me the job on recommendation - he always managed to get me these last minute gigs. I was trying to get out of the labouring trade but there just seemed to be nothing else about at the moment. Nothing that I fancied anyway. I wanted something a bit better for myself, but somehow always ended up exactly back where I started wondering how I'd got there.

I could feel the wet of my T-shirt clinging to me, all white and heavy. It felt nice and fucking irritating all at the same time. Like a soggy hug from your best mate.

I'd thought about going to college and studying to be a chef or something. Catering, I think the course was called, but the course leader bloody hated me. Well, I say she hated me. I think she was more annoyed that I didn't fancy her. She was this fit forty odd year old woman. She really was fit, but I've never been able to keep it up for older women. I don't know why; just always feels like I'm shagging my mum - not ideal.

My trainers were slapping the wet pavements making drips of mud slip up my legs like tiny pieces of shit. To say I felt disgusting would be a complete understatement.

I got to the building site around quarter past six. Fifteen minutes late on the first day isn't too bad I suppose. I could blame delays on the tube or something; no-one would know any different.

I trampled onto the mud and gravel littering the ground at the entrance to the site. Big mesh gates shivering either side of me while the slap of the puddles fought against the patter of rain. Just to the right of the entrance stood a six foot security guard scowling inside his hut, giving me the eye through his half open window.

We exchanged a few words and he pointed me in the direction of a hut about twenty meters down the site.

I opened the door, pushing myself into the shelter of the blue grey sanctuary. A wave of heat met my wet skin and made me want to vomit. Either that or those vodka and cokes were repeating on me. I let the bile settle in my stomach, then turned to see a room full of blokes in high-vis, scattered around in various states of boredom.

"Dan?" A bald bloke with shoulders the size of dumbbells was walking over to me with a clipboard.

"For my sins." I shook out my jacket and pulled my hood down, letting myself drip all over the dirty laminate floor, "sorry I'm late."

"Don't worry, we're running late anyway. Fucking rain."

"Tell me about it." I signalled to the ocean sliding down my clothes.

"Grab a cuppa and dry off. I'll come get you when we work out where you'll be."

"Thanks mate."

I managed to get myself a hot drink and made my way to huddle over by the radiator at the far side of the room. I knew it'd be no hassle me being late. No way anyone's gonna get any work done today anyway; not unless that rain lets up - not likely.

I took off my jacket and hung it over the radiator.

Leaving me stood there with my soaking wet T-shirt clinging to my chest, my tattoos starting to show through the fabric - it would dry eventually.

About ten minutes later and the bald bloke came back over to me, "You feeling dry?"

"As dry as I'm gonna get."

"Listen, don't think it's likely we're gonna have any work for you today."

I bristled for a moment, then came back with, "You what?"

"Sorry mate, not the day for it. Rain makes it unsafe."

"You're still gonna pay me?"

He paused a moment and looked over his shoulder with a twitch, "Sorry mate."

"Fucking ridiculous." I spat, "I could have had a days work elsewhere! I lose a days money cause your lot can't handle the rain."

"Alright mate, calm down."

I grabbed my jacket and slid it on to me, feeling the damp scrape across my arms, "Oh yeah, calm down. I'll do that, mate, yeah. Just cozy up in my penthouse with some champagne and calm down, I will."

I made my way out through the door and back in the torrential rain still hammering onto the brown grey of the ground. Couldn't fucking believe it, Ben always managed to set me up with these bullshit gigs. What type of dickheads don't pay after dragging me all the way down here at the crack of dawn?

I had no idea what to do with myself when I got out of the building site and back onto the pavement. Managed to huddle myself under a red awning from the nearby off-license. The smell of day old fruit and veg mingling with the rain. My life was really going well.

I lay in bed feeling sorry for myself - after finally making it home, soaking wet, I managed to fall into bed and hadn't moved for most of the day. I could still smell the damp smell of rainwater rotting in the corner of my room.

I grasped at the bedside table where my phone was balancing on the edge, white wire dangling down to the plug socket extension. I grabbed my phone and scrolled through the socials - as always there was bollock all of any interest. I flicked over to my mobile banking app, checking the damage of another day without any money coming in and plenty of money going out.

The rain outside was still pouring down, scraping itself against the windows of the tower block making me feel like I was in a siege. Held hostage by Mother Nature.

57p, that's all I had left in the world. A rich man would be jealous of my wealth. I switched over to WhatsApp and pulled up my conversation with Ben. I began to type, "Job today was a complete washout mate. I'm utterly fucked."

I didn't really expect him to do anything about it. I was beyond angry and had landed at completely fucking fucked off.

A few minutes later I got a text back, "Sorry mate."

Great, that makes it all better. I managed to haul myself out of bed and padded out to the kitchen. I hated the patting sound my feet always made on the laminate.

I grabbed myself a cuppa and stood by the window staring out into the London skyline. Well, I say skyline, all I could really see were the blocks of flats opposite mine. Sleek metal running down every edge - I should have been building one of those today. Instead, I was stood there gawping at someone else's work.

Surely there had to be something more to life than all this? I felt like a complete failure. I remember leaving school feeling like life was going to be different for me - I wasn't gonna be a complete waster like my Dad. Yet here I was. But I guess, at least I was trying.

Maybe I should go back to college and do that catering course. At least being a chef I won't get rained off.

Laying on the table was a spliff from the night before, I was tempted to relax and take a drag. But that would be me fucked for the day. Did I want to be fucked for the day? Probably yes, but I was clawing on to the last thread of Hope that I wasn't a complete loser. Spending money I didn't have getting stoned instead of actually doing something in the world.

Not that the world cared.

I stood there for a good half an hour rifling through my brain and resisting the urge to self induce a cannabis coma.

I peered down into the street with diffused vision, not really looking at anything, when a yellow car came into my vision. I whispered, "yellow car" to myself and imagined punching someone stood next to me. But there was no one to punch.

Then I realised - the rain had stopped. Blue was tearing its way through the clouds.

For an instant everything felt lighter.

Fuck it, I thought. I'm going to actually do something.

Chapter 2

Oh my goodness the sky felt light.

"Sorry mate, there's nothing we can get you doing. Everyone has gone home for the day." He stared at me with a mixture of admiration and bewilderment.

"C'mon man, I'm here, get me to do some shovelling or something. Anything. You don't want to waste a days labor. I'll do it for half pay even. Just give me something."

"It's nearly three anyway mate. No point getting you on anything now. Come back tomorrow and I'm sure we'll have something for you."

The more he refused the more my feet dug into the dirt of the building site. I was not going anywhere until I'd earned at least one quid today. "C'mon mate, I'm throwing myself at you here; surely there's something needs doing?"

"See you tomorrow morning. I'm punching out for the day." He began to walk off towards the security hut at the entrance of the site.

I couldn't believe it; I'd spent more money another tube journey down here and still had nothing to show for it. Was I that much of a fucking turd that he wouldn't even let me work for next to nothing? I was taking it too personal. He clearly just wanted to get home early and didn't want to be stuck supervising some dickhead while he digs a few holes, or lays a few bricks.

It was alright for him, probably had a sweet little missus and a dog to get home to. What did I have? You know the answer to that: I had nothing.

My head hung down; the dirt on my boots waving at me. Little bits of stone were sticking into the mud like sprinkles on an ice cream, except less appetising.

This was defeat.

No it fucking wasn't.

Yes, it definitely was.

"I might have some work for you." A soft posh voice pushed itself across the mud and stones. I looked around and saw a suit stood there, staring at me. He looked out of place, the black of his leather shoes floating on the gravel and dirt. His hair was slightly quiffed and his eyes were cut like diamonds. A ring of black sucked the white blue pigments into a spiral.

I just stood there.

"I said I've got some work, I could do with some help in the office. Might not be what you're used to, but it'll pay the bills for a few days."

Where did he even appear from? One moment I was stood in the grey mud on my own, the next he was stood there, hands gently resting on his hips; staring at me with a slight impatience.

"I've not got all day mate, I'd rather not be stood out here in the cold. I'll be in that hut over there if you're up for it."

No way was I built for an office job.

Paper. So much bloody paper I could barely breath. Pages and pages, spread out in every bloody corner of the room. This is why I never wanted to work in an office. Paper makes no sense: it's just endless sheets of useless information that have no bearing on reality. Bricks I can understand; put one on top of the other and build a house - nothing more simple than that.

I don't know how many hours I'd been sat there sifting through that fucking paper.

Tom his name was. He was a suit brought in to sort out the bureaucracy. Apparently there had been some dodgy dealings going on with the planning permission and the finances. I didn't really understand what he was saying most of the time, but it sounded like someone was in serious trouble; he was quite stressed about it.

He'd haul up a a pile of documents onto the desk and sort through; every time he found something he didn't like, he'd shake his head silently and run his fingers through his quiff - his eyes cutting holes in the paper.

Something about being sat there in the heat of the port-a-cabin, made me want to scream. I could feel my blood going stale from the putrid smell of busy work. The edges of my skin started to feel fuzzy and my eyes could barely focus on the sheets.

Every now and then he'd place his pen on the table, his hands would slink up behind his head and he'd lean back into a stare; his eyes tickling across the room to me, saying a little hello. He looked nervous and the slight squint of his eyelids betrayed a curiosity. He was a curiosity to me: he actually seemed to be enjoying this work. I could feel the buzz of electric through his muscles every time he learned something new; every time a new document found it's rightful place in the order of things.

There was something quite sweet about him. He was a strange little filing elf with a twinkle in his thigh. Eye. Why was I looking between his legs? Fucking hell I must have been bored.

"How long you been doing this?" I opted for small talk.

He smirked at me, "Only about two years, I'm still fresh. What about you?"

"Well, I don't really do this. Just doing odd jobs to earn some money, but I always seem to end up doing manual labour."

"You've got the body for it I suppose." The words fell out and then he realised what he'd said. He looked uncomfortable for a second. But only one second, then that awkward squirm transformed into a strange arrogance. What was his game?

"Yeah, well, I suppose you've got to use what God gave you. You've clearly got the brains. I couldn't deal with paperwork all day." I replied.

"Nah, it's easy really. The paper tells you everything you need to know. Just got to look for it and help it find its place."

"Exactly, just one afternoon looking at this shit and I wanna jump off a building." I had a weird admiration for him, but could feel my stomach turning at the look he was giving me. I wanted to run. Where did I want to run to? If I knew that, I probably would have done it.

I could feel the blood rushing through me, pumping through my veins like a torrent. My balls gave out a heat. Sweat started to gather on them and all I could think about was his tongue licking it all off.

Fuck.

What the fuck was this?

He looked at his watch, then back at me. Holding my stare, like a big cat wanting to pounce. Then he spoke, "Are you free to come back tomorrow?"

"Yeah, I guess so. Not sure I'll be that much use to you though mate. I don't have a clue what I'm doing."

"You're doing great. There's not a lot to it honestly."

"Easy for you to say. I don't have your education."

His eyes rested on me and he seemed to consider my words carefully.

"Well, honestly I wouldn't pin your hopes on labouring here. Between you and me the site is probably going to get shut down. They don't have planning permission for the works here, so it's only a matter of time before the council closes in and issues an enforcement notice." He picked up his pen from the desk and started fiddling with it.

"Well that's fine, I'll just find another site. This is just to tide me over anyways."

"That's fine, but if this place has to be closed the construction company will probably go bust. So it'll be a while before any big projects are happening in the area."

"So what you're saying is, I'm fucked?"

He sucked in a breath of air and showed his teeth, "Well you'll be alright. Like you said this is just to ride you over right? You've got bigger things on the horizon."

That felt like a slap around the face. He didn't think I was capable of shit. Talking to me like some idiot with no more than two brain cells to rub together.

"I don't need to be here, mate." I said as my tattooed muscles tensed.

His face recoiled slightly, "I wasn't taking the piss. I'm just saying things could wrap up here really quick if you're not careful."

"I don't need your advice mate. I'm not some scrubber." The look of him there in his suit ignited a fire in my gut.

The muscles in his face relaxed and the brown of his hair stood stone still. I could hear a slight bristle from his blazer rubbing against his shirt, but that was it. The rest of the room sat silent. His eyelids closed slowly, then opened, before his body hunched back over the paper on the desk and our interaction was over.

* * *

Chapter 3

The sun was about to burst.

My hi-vis jacket was rubbing against my nipples, moving the sweat that was clinging to my hairs. My tongue was dry and my thighs were soaking. Everything was the wrong way around.

I'd been driving this digger to and fro all morning. Feeling the heat intensifying as the sun stretched higher into the sky. I didn't know how much longer I could last before melting into a puddle on the ground. Mounts of dirt sitting like lead in the oversized metal shovel and then dripping slowly down like lava as I pulled the lever towards me.

Even watching the mud and grit pour out made me think of running water. What I wouldn't give to be sat on the beach with a bottle of beer watching the curves of the sea reflecting bikini'd asses into my eyes. My cock twinged slightly against my tight white underwear, the sweat creating even more friction.

Luckily I'd managed a few days work on the site since my day in the office. Things were starting to look up and there was at least a chance I might be able to pay my rent this month. The world was looking that much brighter.

The site manager came into view to my right. His hard helmet was slipping around on his bald sweaty head. He was waving his arms at me, signaling for me to stop the digger.

I twisted the key in the ignition and the digger rumbled to a stop. My ears were ringing from the sudden silence.

He jogged awkwardly up to the cabin door. A weird smile was on his mouth, but it didn't match the look in his eyes.

"Everything alright mate?" I asked.

"Oh yeah, all good. All good. Just - can we have a little chat?"

"Yeah, I'm free as a bird" I chuckled. The heat from the sun was sticking to me. I jumped down from the cabin and made my way down to eye level with Mark, "what's up?"

He stared at me. A little bit of sweat trickling down his stubble. "Listen mate, really sorry about this, but we're going to have to let you go."

"What do you mean you've got to let me go?"

19

"I mean we can't have you working here. Sorry mate."

A ribbon of anger knotted in my gut. I looked in his eyes trying to work out if this was some sort of joke. His eyes twitched with a nervousness that could only be real. Another bead of sweat licked his cheek. What was he so worried about?

"Mind telling me why?" I asked.

"Well, it's nothing personal, it's just we're having to make cut backs. We're well over budget for this project. The council keep fucking us over with the planning permission delays."

"Don't give me that, your mate in the office told me that you ain't even bothering with planning permission."

"Well my mate in the office doesn't know what he's talking about. He's just a jobs-worth trying to justify his pay check."

I shifted from one foot to the other.

"Mate, I need the money from this job. You know how hard it is to get on a project these days? Even government projects are being cut left right and centre. I need some way to put food on the table."

"Listen, I really am sorry. There's nothing I can do about it. We can pay you for the rest of the day, but that will have to be it."

"Forget about it mate, I don't need this bullcrap." I tugged my hi-vis from my torso and stuffed it into his arms. It felt good to let my skin breath properly. I started off with intention to the site exit - the third time I was stomping away from this place in anger.

Then I remembered my last attempted walk out of here. I remembered Tom, sitting in that office, surrounded by paper. I remembered the way his suit trousers hugged his asscheeks. Why was I thinking about his asscheeks? He offered to let me come back and work with him, but I'd refused. Being around him made me so uncomfortable - I couldn't escape the feeling that he had the hots for me. Who could blame the poor guy?

Maybe it wouldn't be too bad to go work with him. He seemed like I nice guy, maybe I'd just have to lay down the law and make it clear that I wasn't interested in him in that way. Diffuse and tension straight away so we could just get on with working. I didn't really have much of a choice. How else was I gonna make enough to pay rent this month?

Alright, that decided it - I had to at least ask him if the job was still on offer. What else did I have to lose? I'm sure I could cope with fending off a harmless little gay boy for a few weeks while I earned some crumb.

Next minute I found myself marching into the port-a-cabin where he'd been working. The place was empty. Most of the paperwork was neatly packed away and the place looked like it hadn't been touched that day. Come to think of it, I didn't remember seeing him come into work this morning. Not that I was really paying much attention to what he was up to. Why would I?

Well fuck, maybe he'd finished what he needed to do?

I dropped into the security desk at the front.

"Alright fella? Don't suppose you've seen that Tom bloke today have you? The accountant guy." I asked the security guard.

"Nah mate, he's all finished up. Think he sorted it all."

"Oh right, no worries."

I made my way to the gate. I could feel my skin hardening and a drip of black oil spreading out in my stomach. What was I going home to? Nothing. My life was empty. Tom would be in his cushy little town house sipping on a G&T most likely. Prick.

There was a twitch in my groin.

I found myself leaning back towards the security guard.

"Don't suppose you've got his number have you?"

"Data protection mate, can't just hand information out."

"He won't mind, he was meant to give it me, but he forgot."

Chapter 4

"Thanks for coming over like this."

I couldn't believe I'd ended up in this position.

"Don't mention it." And I really meant that. As grateful as I was to be able to earn a little of bit of money. That I was earning it under these circumstances meant I'd really rather not think about it. I pushed the saw to a fro; sawdust flew up into the air and stuck to the sweat forming on my skin.

He kept standing there silently grinning over me. Why did he look so pleased with himself? Like somehow he'd gotten his way.

"You sure I can't get you a drink?" he said.

"You got a lemonade or something? I could go for something sweet like that."

"Yeah sure, I think I've got some in the fridge, nice and cool for you."

He spun and wandered back into the house leaving me to construct his decking like the mug I was. Talk about going up in the world. I now found myself some lackey doing DIY for an early twenties graduate nob end. This was so bloody degrading. But it was only two more days till rent was due and I was still no where near being able to pay it.

I finished cutting a plank into size and slotted it onto the decking, making sure the edges lined up perfect. If I was forced to work like a dog just to live at least I could try and make a quality product. I suppose it wasn't ideal but there could be the chance of making a business out of this. Not that I really wanted to be a self employed handy man. Didn't exactly give me much of a future to look forward too. I saw what labouring did to my Grandad. His body was absolutely knackered by the time he was fifty.

That would be me, another shell of a man to come out of this family. All I wanted was try and make something of myself in this world. Why did that feel so hard? Here was this Tom guy, clearly worked hard for sure. But he has everything that I want, how the hell did he get there already? This place is got is no mansion, but it's nice. It's his. What more can a man ask for than a place of his own? Some comfort and some security. Somewhere he can build a family.

Build a family. Fat chance of that happening for me when I can't even look after myself. What woman would be interested in a guy like me?

"Here you go. Don't drink it too fast." He was so bloody happy. He didn't have any right to be that happy.

"Listen," he said, "I know this probably isn't ideal for you. I know you're a proud guy and you probably have higher ideals in mind that building my decking for me. But you're clearly a clever guy. You'll work it out."

"I'm fine mate."

"Yeah, I know you're fine. I'm just..." He looked at me, he wanted to say something, but I'm not sure even he could work out what it was. "Just, thank you. That's all. I appreciate it. I know it might look like I've got it made here. But it's pretty bloody lonely actually. The thought of doing this decking all on my own and coming back here night after night to no-one is kind of driving me a bit mad. Can't even manage to get any mates round. I think everyone kind of feels a bit intimidated ever since I started to make some money. Like they're jealous or something. I mean, I don't even earn that much. I've just been really lucky. My Nan died last year so I got a bit of inheritance to get a mortgage on this place."

I kept my gaze on him. He was sweet. Was he trying to say he wanted to be my mate?

"I get it mate. Don't worry. People can be really fickle about stuff. I'm sure you'll make some new mates. Or maybe when they get older and get a bit more sorted they'll realise they were being dicks. Unless they end up like me." I let out an exasperated laugh.

"You're doing great man. It's not an easy world to make your way in. There's a lot of luck involved."

"Yeah."

"Listen, why don't you give it a rest for the day?"

"Can't really afford to mate. I need to get the hours in. I'd rather just get the job finished."

"I'll pay you for the rest of the day. Just relax."

"I don't need charity."

I continued hammering a nail into a piece of wood,

securing it into place. One more piece on what was turning out to be a bloody beautiful bit of decking. I stuck my hand into a tub of nails, grabbing for another bolt of metal to hammer into place. As my hand was wriggling around inside the tub I felt a sharp tug. My hand was ripped from the tub and I was left with a gently scratching feeling on my skin.

I stared at him. He was smirking at me. "Can't finish up work if you've run out of nails."

What was that look on his face? I felt myself flush. My blood banging on the inside of my skin. "Funny game."

"I don't know what you're talking about." He walked off, proudly cradling the tub of nails in his arms and disappeared into the house.

"So come on then, don't be shy. What's the dream?" He asked me.

"The dream is to not have to be in a constant state of stress over where my next meal is coming from." I laughed and took another sip of beer. I'd spent the last hour or two sat on the leather couch in Tom's living room, chatting away and perhaps finally starting to relax."

"Well that's an obvious answer. Come on, we're friends aren't we? You can tell me for real. What is it you really want from your life?"

"Jeez, what kind of a question is that? How is anyone supposed to actually answer it? How am I supposed to know what I actually want? I've got no time to think about questions as important as that. And I certainly don't have the brains to think about it."

"You've got more brains than you think you have. You're not just some muscle-head. I mean for one, your muscle is a bit lacking."

I leaned over from my seat and smacked him on the arm. "Fuck off, got more muscle than you you skinny little prick." We both laughed into our drinks.

"I don't really think the world is set up to make people more clever. I mean, who does it benefit to get you educated?"

"I'm not oppressed, Tom. Just trying to do my best."

We slowly sipped again on our drinks and a moment of stillness settled into the room. The laminate floor and the high ceilings echoing the awkward moment. Both our legs spread wide, his bare feet gripping into the floor. God I felt alone. I should leave, what was I doing here with this guy? We were from completely different worlds. He was just taking pity on me. He felt sorry for me. Poor working class bloke not even able to afford a bottle of beer.

"I feel oppressed." He said.

"What do you mean you feel oppressed? You got it good here mate."

"I don't really know what I mean. Don't worry. Probably just the beer."

A key turned in the lock and suddenly the door swung open. In chimed the sound of high heels clattering against the floor.

Tom sprung up, "Shit. Mum I told you not to just walk in!" He ran the the hallway, his feet slipping slightly on the floor.

"Well if you didn't want me to pop in you shouldn't have given me a key." I couldn't see here, but I could hear her voice. Middle class with razors in her throat.

"I didn't want to give you a key. You insisted."

"No need to be like that Tom. Are you okay? Didn't like the thought of you being here alone so I thought I'd pop in." As she said it the light brown of her hair flew past the doorway and she caught my gaze. She saw the high viz laying beside me and the stubble on my chin. I could see her nose crinkle into a slight grimace that she was desperate to suppress. "Oh hello. You're not alone."

"No I'm not alone. Can you go please?"

"It's alright. I'll get out of your hair." I piped up, slowly pushing up on my thighs and setting my beer to rest on the table beside me. He looked distraught.

"Dan it's fine. Sit down."

"No honestly, I need to get off anyway. Don't want to take up your whole evening." His Mum kept her gaze on me. She had the same blue eyes as him but hers were far less kind.

"Don't leave on my account. A friend of Tom's is a friend of mine, or are you just here doing some work?" She glanced again at the high vis jacket in my hands, at the tattoos rolling up my arms. My skin still coated in a layer of sawdust.

"Just been here working for the day, Miss. Tom was nice enough to offer me drink to thank me for my work."

"It's only four o'clock." She remarked. He teeth clamped together. "Well I suppose you deserve it, it's difficult work you have to do. Is this for the decking?" She turned to Tom.

"Yeah, Dan is a mate from work who's agreed to help out with the decking. Tom replied. "I was going to do it myself, but I was a bit out of my depth."

I couldn't stand the maternal tension sucking the life from the room.

"Alright, well see you tomorrow mate," I said. And with that I was out of the door and away.

* * *

Chapter 5

I shouldn't have done it. But I didn't know what else to do with myself. I was so goddamn confused. Everything was hazy. The air was tight. There was a weird fuzz about the room that told me it was either the middle of the night, or I was dead. I don't know which I'd have preferred.

I could smell perfume running down the back of my throat, sticking to my tonsils, making the saliva scrape as I swallowed. I looked over to my left and there she was. Blonde hair tangled in the pillow and wrapped around my fingers. I'd fucked her. In a drunken haze, I'd fucked her until I didn't know who I was anymore. It was good to have my end away. But I wanted to be anywhere but next to her right now.

I reached around with my other hand grasping for my phone. I could feel my foreskin was sore against the sheets as I moved, turning over towards the blaring blue light of the screen: 2:04am. There was a text bubble on the screen, but I couldn't take it in. Fuck sake, where even was I?

The sight of her made me feel sick. The memory of her moaning as I slid in and out of her made me sick. I remembered her flattering me, her stupid giggle, the way she ran her hands along my muscles. The cold flirtation that somehow convinced me that we had some connection. We had no connection. She didn't want to be near me, she just wanted to ride someone, to feel some pleasure, to have some fun with the guy she thought I was.

I moved as slow as I could and slid out from the covers. Maybe she wouldn't hear. Maybe I could escape without having to look in her eyes and know full well that I had no interest in her. I didn't give a shit about her, about her life, about her feelings. She was just a piece of meat to me in that moment. I just wanted to feel a bit of human warmth and she was the closest and easiest thing nearby.

I escaped and I was out into the world.

The air was crisp. Yellows reflecting off the black concrete as I huddled into my coat and tried to push down the bile bubbling in my stomach. My throat was constricting and all I could hear in my head was the voice of my Mum. I wanted her to tell me off. She didn't care enough to even tell me I was a dick head. She didn't give a shit about me.

Tom's cared too much. I didn't know which was worse.

Tom.

My hand ripped my phone from my pocket and I saw his name on the screen. I slid my finger along and read. *Hope you're okay mate. Anytime you need a chat, you know where I am.*

The black feeling in my gut lifted slightly. It was strange to feel like someone really cared. Why did Tom care? I was just some bloke. He was just lonely, why would he give a shit about me?

I hoped he was alright, his Mum seemed like a right

battleaxe. I'd just bolted and left him to it. He was one of the few people who was actually nice to me these days. Nice. Who the fuck was I kidding? Why was I worried about people being nice to me? The world isn't a nice place, it's a fucking miserable place. All I want is some warmth and some comfort but the world feels cold and it feels harsh. There I was in the middle of the night, in the middle of the street, the smell of piss floating from the corner of a building. This wasn't some beautiful experience. This was meaningless and cold.

But Tom was warm.

I walked past the construction site. It was completely empty, the security guard didn't even seem to be there. I guess with the project going under they'd just jumped ship. No one around to pay for security.

Something took hold of me and suddenly my hands were gripping the fence vaulting me over into the gravelly darkness.

Surrounding me were the half finished remains of my work. The work of hundreds of other blokes all working together to build something. To bring something into the world that wasn't there before. But it went wrong and now there was just rubble and dirt and a few empty skeletons.

I wandered around the site, somehow feeling more content than I had been in years. Something about feeling like that space was mine, the building site was mine, the raw potential was mine.

I climbed up to the top of the half built block of flats and took in the scenery. The glow of the sleeping city. It was even colder up there, but somehow that bothered me less. I felt free. That's all I wanted. I just wanted to build a life for myself, to be able to construct my own world and share it with some people that I loved.

I sat down and felt the space beside myself. I didn't want to be alone up here. I didn't want to be alone anywhere.

I pulled out my phone and my fingers did the work for me.

"Yeah, she is quite the character." Tom said. He was leaning his back against the bags of concrete that had been left to rot.

"Seems like she cares a lot about you though mate. That's something to be grateful for." I replied.

"Yeah, I am grateful. I know not everyone has a family, let alone one that loves them. But she's been even worse since Dad died. Like she's got no life of her own so she wants to run mine for me. I just wish she'd live a life for herself. She spent her whole life looking after dad and me and now she doesn't know what to do with herself. And she's just so fucking uptight."

"Well trust me. It's better than the alternative. My mum just spends her life high off her tits smoking weed. I'm not sure she's really even aware that I exist."

He didn't quite know how to respond. But his eyes seemed to fold back on themselves like he was falling into the depths of himself. "I know you exist." He said.

I don't know why I thought of him when I was sat up there. Something about the space of the city rooftops in front of me was quieting something inside me. But when there was quiet, I felt like I wanted him there in the quiet with me. What was happening to me? I suppose I'd never really had a proper mate before. I'd never really felt like someone saw anything in me more than what was there on the surface. All people saw was a bit of muscle and some tattoos. He saw something else.

"And what is it that you see mate?" I asked. His head withdrew slightly and he bared his teeth. The smoothness of his skin wrinkling as he smiled. His pupils looked like bullet holes. Shots fired.

"I see a good guy, trying his best. You're obviously much more sensitive and clever than you've ever been able to express."

"Sensitive?" I bristled.

"Yes, sensitive. The tattoos don't fool me. I just mean you're intelligent, you look at the world in a certain way. You can see details that other people can't see. And things affect you. You deal with it so well, but I think you've been keeping it from yourself cause there's nowhere for it to go. No one to share it with."

"Alright Posh boy don't get too deep. You're a weird guy you know."

"I am?"

"Yeah, I've never felt like this around someone

before. I mean, The people I grew up around were completely different. Can't quite work out why you're so nice to me."

"I'm not saying it to be nice. I just respect you. Just cause we come from different backgrounds. It doesn't really mean anything." He stared into my eyes and I could feel something in me stir. I wanted to touch him. I wanted to hold him. What was this? What was he doing to me?

"Can I be honest with you?" I said, noticing the cold of the concrete pressing into my thigh muscles.

"I'd be annoyed if you weren't."

I waited a moment and noticed a wisp of hair flying out from his temple. A slight red glow to his cheek.

"I feel different around you. For some reason I feel like I can trust you and…" I could feel a wrench in my stomach. I wanted to speak and tell him the truth, but I was terrified. Once the words had slipped out, there was no putting them back in. No pretending they didn't exist. They'd become their own force independent in the world.

"And?"

There was a tickle of dry skin on his lips. His mouth

was slightly parted, I could see the slick of his tongue resting against the back of his teeth. Before I knew what I was doing my head had moved forwards and all I could see were his eyes floating closer until our lips were touching.

I pressed my lips into him and felt the soft cushion of his skin against mine. Liquid gold melted in my gut. My tongue pushed through and gently stroked against his, as my hand softly stroked the back of his head. His hair was smooth on my fingers, his tongue wet in my mouth. My stubble rubbed against his chin, but he didn't seem to mind. He just kept kissing me in return, his body giving itself to me. His warmth flooding through my body.

The pace quickened, then slowed, then stopped. We sat licking our lips and staring into each other's eyes. I couldn't believe what I'd done. But I didn't regret one second of it. Suddenly I felt alive.

He smiled at me for a second, then his face changed and he said, "Listen, I should probably tell you something."

Chapter 6

I swung the pick axe down into the ground, hearing the crunch of gravel and stone. It stuck there, wedged in the ground as my muscles tended in an attempt to pull it back out. I groaned, pulling again with all of my might only for it to stick more firmly.

"Fuck!" I cursed. My arms were shaking as if they could not hold me up. I needed to get this thing out before it crushed my toes.

I couldn't believe that Tom hadn't told me. I knew he liked me. That kiss was something else. So how did I end up stuck in a dirt hole, being beaten by a fucking pick axe? What had happened between us?

The answer came to me when he walked up next to me, grinning like a madman. I need help! Tom hasn't done anything wrong, he was just trying to help a friend. Why did it annoy me so much?

I let out another growl of frustration, trying once again to get the stupid thing off the ground.

Tom chuckled softly. "You alright? You look like you're about to give yourself an aneurism."

"Yeah, I'm fine." I replied, my words dripping with

sarcasm.

The decking was nearly done, I just needed to make a few more holes for the posts and it would be done. What would I do then? Try and find another site to work on I suppose. There wasn't anything wrong with that. Even though it wasn't what I wanted.

Tom was just looking down at the mess that I had created.

We'd not spoken properly since last night. He'd confessed something to me that I really had seen coming and I don't know why it upset me so much.

Apparently his best friend was pregnant with his baby. She really wanted a kid and him being Gay he figured he'd never be able to have his own kids. I don't know why, but when he told me that, I completely freaked out. I ran straight out of the contrstruction site and ran home.

But I turned up at Tom's again this morning and acted like none of it had happened.

"It looks like you lost your damn job mate." Tom joked, looking me over.

He's right. The tool was wedged into the soil so hard that even when I pulled it back out, the top part was still buried in the ground.

I was so confused about this whole situation, I'd never been interested in guys before, but that kiss with him last night was something else. And looking at him again now made my stomach flip.

I wanted to have kids of my own, I wanted to have a family. I couldn't have a relationship with a guy and let go of all that. Especially not with a guy who had his own kid. It was too weird. Too confusing.

I couldn't help but think of his lips against mine. How soft they felt. How warm. How good. And it didn't help that he looked damn sexy in his tattered jeans.

And those blue eyes. They made things much clearer.

Tom leaned down and tried to pull the end of the pickaxe out of the ground. He tugged as hard as he could but it still wouldn't budge. he turned to me a gave a little lau "Well, I guess we're going to be here awhile."

I stood there staring at him, a bit dumbfounded, watching him work. It was kind of cute actually. I couldn't help myself. I wanted another kiss.

His face scrunched up in concentration while he

struggled with the pickaxe. He pushed himself harder, digging deeper into the ground.

When the tip of the pick finally broke through the surface, Tom let out a loud sigh of relief. Then he took a step back and wiped his brow.

I immediately grabbed him and pushed my tongue into his mouth. His hands found their way around my waist and he pulled me closer. I moaned as our tongues clashed together.

My hand gripped his hair tightly, tugging a little. He responded by pushing me against the pickaxe handle, making me gasp for breath. When I managed to regain control of my breathing, we relaxed into a gently rhythm, rubbing our tongues together and letting our bodies melt into each other.

When we finally stopped he said, "listen, I know this is probably new for you. I'm sure you've never been with a guy before, I understand if it brings up lots of weird emotions. But we don't have to do anything you don't want to."

I smiled, pressing myself against him. This was all new "I want to try... but I need to think about what this means."

He nodded, kissing me again. I put both hands on his cheeks and kissed him back, slowly moving my hands down to rest on his chest. My cock was growing harder than I think it had ever been before.

As if sensing the direction my thoughts had gone in, Tom began to move his hips. For a posh boy he was really eager. Our lips broke apart and I gasped for air.

"Shall we take a break? Can't do much now the pickaxe is broken." Tom said.

I nodded, following him in, not wanting to let go of his warmth yet.

When we got inside Tom led me gently to the sofa, never taking his hands off of me. My cock was throbbing through my jeans the whole time, my sweat sticking to my T-shirt. As soon as I sat down on the couch he went and grabbed a towel from the bathroom. He brought it over and handed it to me before he stood up again, looking at me.

"I'll be back in a few minutes."

I nodded but did not speak. The room was silent aside from my heavy breathing and even that was getting harder by the second. When he finally left the room I let out a sigh, placing my head into my hands. The silence seemed to get louder as time passed, my heart beating faster. I could feel my pants starting to get wetter as my rod grew and seeped precum.

When he finally walked back into the room he had two glasses of water. He passed one to me and waited for me to take a sip. He stood in front of me smiling, then when I was done, he took the glass from my hands, placed it on the coffee table and gently straddled me. His legs wrapping either side of my thighs.

I could tell how hard he was, because he kept

rubbing himself against me. As he started moving his hips I felt myself losing control, and the moment I looked up at him, his eyes were filled with desire and lust. As if he knew what I was thinking he leaned forward and kissed me. My hand grabbed around to squeeze his ass cheeks as he rocked backwards and forwards on top of my hardness. His ass felt firm and pert. God it felt good.

He pulled his face away and looked at me, then his hands slid down and started unbuttoning my trousers.

I wanted to protest, but something told me that this would be good. Something about the innocence posh boy face doing something so dirty made me even hornier. And sure enough, when he undid my trousers the sound of my zipper sliding down made us both shudder and moan.

His fingers slowly pushed my boxers down, revealing my dick. He smiled wickedly and looked at me, his eyes sparkling with excitement.

"You ready?"

My only reply was to nod as he lowered his lips to my dick. His mouth gently licked and sucked on my shaft until I felt myself being consumed by the wetness of his mouth.

I had never been so turned on in my life. It felt like my cock was plunging into heaven.

He wrapped his hands around my balls as his head started to bob up and down on my hardness. He stopped momentarily and shot his blue eyes in my direction. Giving me a smile. He took another big lick of my dick then returned his attention back to sucking on it. As he moved to go lower he caught my eye once more. I gave him a smirk before biting down lightly on my bottom lip. I saw his eyes darken as he continued his ministrations. All I could think about was how good it would feel to cum all over his face and mouth. To watch his blushing red cheeks dripping with my seed. And then, I could feel my climax building. I felt like I was going to explode any minute now.

"Oh my god! Ahh!!!" I screamed as my orgasm built. He kept his mouth on me, never stopping his rhythmic movements. I held onto his neck, trying desperately to keep my grip, while my other hand clenched around the cushions underneath. I felt the hot liquid leaking out of me but didn't care; I couldn't see anything, the world was spinning too fast. Then as suddenly as it came, warmth spread throughout every inch of my body.

As my panting began to slow I noticed the ceiling fan lightly spinning over head. Who on Earth had ceiling fans these days? Then my gaze met his as he slowly rose from between my legs, licking his lips. He had swallowed every drop of me. I lay there spent while he stood before me like a proud lion after feasting on its prey.

"Sorry." I said.

"Don't be."

"I didn't get to help you out."

"Don't worry, there's plenty of time for that. You enjoy yourself." He leant down and kissed me on the forehead while I drifted into a whole other world. The sweat from my ass cheeks creating friction between me and the leather sofa. My eyes began to close. I was gone.

Chapter 7

I'm not sure how it happened. But there I was, in bed with him. I had his legs wrapped around mine. My skin sinking into him. I could feel the hairs on his chin tickling against my arm. I'd never been like this with a man before. I wasn't sure I'd ever been like that with anyone before.

There was a bit of rain drizzling outside, tapping on the pavement, sliding down the windows. The curtains were open, letting the light slip in. It was the white grey light of a cloudy day. But something about being in bed and warm made the greyness feel whiter

Tom's back expanded into my chest with every breath he took. Then, a whisper of air leaving through his slightly parted mouth.

What was I doing? Was I actually getting into something with a guy, or was this just a shag?

I didn't know anymore, but I knew I didn't want to be anywhere else except right there with him. That's when my heart started pounding, beating faster than it should have, so loud, I thought for sure Tom would hear.

Tom rolled over onto his back, looking up at me. I followed suit. He smiled.

"You don't have to stay if you don't want to," he said, "you can go home. We had a good time but I don't want you to feel like we're married or something!"

I laughed nervously. "No no, I'm good. I'm having a really good time. Just not really sure what to make of it all. Never thought of myself being with a guy. This is brand new territory for me."

"Yeah, I get it. But you're doing great. Can't believe that was the first time you've ever had a cock in your mouth. You knew exactly what to do." He laughed and nudged gently against my back.

"Not a compliment I ever thought I'd want to hear. But I'm glad you liked it. It felt amazing cumming in your mouth."

"You tasted good."

"Sorry I didn't swallow you. I loved sucking you off but the thought of cum in my mouth kind of freaked me out a bit."

He laughed, "Honestly it's fine. As long as I cum I don't mind where it goes." He pushed his hips gently back into my groin. I couldn't help but think about what it might feel like to be inside of him. I bet it was tight. Way tighter than pussy.

"So how are you feeling about being a dad?" The question just fell out of my mouth. I didn't really know where it was coming from. All I wanted was to make him feel comfortable and relaxed. I didn't need to know anything more than that. But it seemed important somehow.

"I don't know, I mean it won't really be my kid. I'm just the sperm, I won't be helping raise it." He replied.

"But it's your best friend you're helping out right? So you will see the kid. Don't you think that will make you feel something? Won't it be weird?"

He tensed, I could feel he hadn't thought it through properly. Or was avoiding thinking about it too deeply. Like the whole subject caused him so much pain that he couldn't quite bear it.

"I'm sorry," I said, "we don't have to talk about it. It's not really any of my business. I guess, I'm just thinking about how I would feel."

"You're right. I should think about these things. Maybe I've been a bit naive to be honest. I just kind of feel so lost and like there isn't much meaning to my life so I thought what the hell! But I don't know if it's really the best thing for me. Or for the poor kid I'm creating." He laughed again, but then went quiet.

The only sound for a while was the wind outside and our breathing. I could feel the muscles in his thighs tighten. I knew he was trying to work out whatever he needed to say. But he didn't need to say anything. The air in the room felt crisp and clean, but my insides felt heavy. I wanted to open a window to bring some more fresh air into the room. But I didn't want to move.

We'd spent the whole morning lazing around together. For some reason, despite not really knowing how I felt about the whole situation, I didn't want to leave just yet. I wanted to be there with him. It was strange for me, this feeling that made my stomach turn and my cheeks flush red. We were still in his room after breakfast, sitting on his bed playing Candy Crush and chatting.

"So would like to do this again some time or do you think it'll be a one time thing?" He asked me.

"I don't know, I mean I'm having a really great time with you. But honestly I don't know what I can offer you. I want a proper relationship. I want something traditional. And I guess I never really saw that as an option with a guy."

"Well I'm quite traditional too. But obviously being Gay kind of makes it hard to fit in with the traditional norms. As much as I think they're important. But I guess…"

He paused and looked really bashful for a moment.

"What is it?" I asked.

"Can I kiss you?"

My heart nearly stopped beating then. I didn't really

know what to say, so I just leaned into him and pressed my lips against his. I could hear his heart thumping wildly against his ribcage and could feel his pulse in his wrist as I grabbed him. His skin was cool and taught.

Instantly I could feel the blood rushing to my groin again. This time I wasn't sure if it was because of what he had said or because of what he was doing. But I wanted more of him. I pulled away from him slightly. The sheets were gently wrapped around our legs, both of us resting in boxers and T-shirts. I could feel the fabric of my underwear stretching as my cock expanded.

He looked at me and smirked before leaning down and kissing me again. This time the kiss was deeper and hungrier. He slid his hand under my T-shirt, running his hand up my chest. I felt him touch my nipple, slowly drawing a circle with his finger. The feeling of his skin against my sent me wild. I grabbed at his ass cheek, enjoying the sensation of my fingers pressing into the fatty cushion.

He groaned softly in between kisses, grinding against me.

He whispered into my lips, "I want you inside me."

I didn't know what to say. If letting him suck me off was new territory, then this was a whole other galaxy. I loved the idea of fucking him, but I didn't want to hurt him. How could he manage taking my cock inside him? How would that feel good?

"Is that really what you want?" I asked.

"Oh God yeah, ever since I saw you on the site that day I've been fantasising about riding you. Especially when you were in that high vis jacket." He grinned and continued to grind his cock against me.

"Doesn't it hurt? Having a cock inside you?"

"Well as long as you go slow with me to start. I'll be fine. Once you're in and I'm relaxed, it feels like nothing else in the world. Trust me."

I looked at his sweet little face. I was reminded of him sat in that office in his shirt and tight little trousers. He was fucking gorgeous and the thought of pounding him was too much to bear.

"Alright, but you might have to show me what to do. Never had my cock in someone's arse before."

"Don't worry, I'll show you how it's done. You just lay there."

In a flash his underwear was off and he was rifling
through the drawers looking for something. Then he
whipped out a condom and some lube and was
straddling me and pulling my boxers down. He had a
condom on me in no time and was slathering me up
with lube. He looked so excited sat there in just a T-
shirt his cock gently throbbing below the line of his
pubic hair.

The next thing I knew he was squatting over me,
the light from the window sliding across his
cheekbones making his eyes spark. He positioned my
cock underneath his hole and slowly began to push
himself down onto me.

"Relax." I heard him whisper. After a few moments
of negotiating his tightness he finally got me
completely in. I was completely consumed in the
warmth of his arsehole and it felt like nothing I could
ever imagine. It felt like I was finally home, like I was in
the place I was meant to be. My cock was made to be
inside this guy.

He tilted his head to the ceiling and what breathing
slow and deep breaths while I just savoured the feeling
of being inside him. Then he started to bounce gently

on my shaft while pumping slowly. At first it hurt a bit because he was so tight, but soon I was lost in it. I watched his cock bouncing in time to the bucking of my hips as I desperately tried to get closer to him.

Tom suddenly lifted himself up, giving me enough room to thrust myself forward, hitting him right in the most sensitive part. I grunted, trying my best to get even closer.

He continued to rock back and forth with his body, getting faster every passing second until he hit his peak. The noises coming out of him were animalistic. I grabbed at his T-shirt, pulling it into a fist as I continued thrusting into him.

Then I could feel the pressure rising in my shaft. "Tom, I can't last much longer."

"Come inside me." he yelped as he stroked himself. "Come for me."

Then I lost control, my bodying was rutting and spawning. Sweat firing from every pore as the light seared my eyes. My balls tightened and pleasure erupted out of me firing into his ass as I grunted like an animal.

I kept thrusting as I emptied myself into him, the

moans from his mouth intensifying as he picked up the speed of his wanking. Then he fired out his load all over my stomach, wet drips of white landing on my skin and T-shirt.

Heavy breathing was the only sound left in the room. The smell of sweat and come the only scent. God this was perfect.

I opened my eyes and met Tom's. He was breathing heavily as if he was trying to catch his breath as well. His hands were still clasped over his cock. We were still for a moment letting the pleasure fully release and for normal consciousness to return. Then he slowly pulled me out of him. Disposed of the come filled condom wrapped around my cock and collapsed in a heap next to me, his arm gently draped across my chest.

"That was fucking incredible." I said.

He laughed in agreement.

"We'll that settles it. I definitely want to do that again!" and with that we slipped off into a satisfied sleep.

The End

Chapter 1

Kevin

There I was. Week five in the middle of butt-fuck nowhere. I don't think I'd ever been so consistently thirsty in my entire fucking life. Every day, all day, my mouth was as dry as a camel's pussy. I'd give anything for a suck on an ice pole or a nice solero or two. Me and the lads spent a lot of summers as kids just sat around on our bikes on any bit of green we could find; eating soleros and shouting at anyone stupid enough to walk by us. We were complete nob ends; it's true, but it was good fun at the time at least. In fact right then, it seemed like that was the best time of my life. But any time of my life was better than that.

It was five weeks since our posting there in the middle of a dessert and absolutely no action to speak of. None. Not even a wild dog to fend off. Just endless sun beating down on us and the odd mirage of a naked beauty coming into view on the horizon; only to find it was one of the scouts coming back from endless patrol of the empty territory around us.

Don't know how many lads were posted there exactly. Maybe one hundred, hard to be sure. With our skins-heads and identical sand brown camos it was hard to actually distinguish us as individual people. Just a bunch of dried up prunes burning in the heat.

I was so excited to finally get there, all them years in training, dreaming of finally getting into the action and doing some good in the world. Something to make all that boredom and bullshit to get there, worth it. But no, just more boredom and bullshit. Only less women; and less rain.

They flew us into this camp cause there was some intel of a rogue militia group nearby that were planning an attack on a local town. I don't know if the intel was dodgy or if they just needed to make up an excuse to make us look busy. But there was certainly no sign of any attack any time soon.

The boys were all going feral. Bored out of their fucking brains and horny as hell with nothing to do with it. The amount of bust-ups over home-brew beer was unreal. They all needed a good night out and a good woman to spend the night with. Cheer 'em up and takes their minds off it. Or at least something to shoot.

Most of 'em came from small towns; they'd never seen more action than a weekend brawl at a local pub. Some old uncle getting too twatted and ending his night getting decked by someone more in his peak. I felt sorry for 'em all. They were even younger than me; and even more hopeful. Ain't easy being a bloke these days. Feels like we're getting blamed for everything; but we're as lost as anyone else. I mean, we must be. Who would choose to go into the field of combat if he was completely happy with his lot. We knew we were just there to fight for someone else's oil. But what else were we supposed to do? Spend our lives flipping burgers to fill someone else's wallet? At least this way we get to pretend we're heroes. Pretend that something still means anything. We knew the truth though. Well, some of us did.

I'd not killed anyone yet, not even had the chance. I didn't know what it would feel like. Maybe I would feel like a hero. Protecting Queen and country. I hoped so.

Mum was livid when I told her I was coming, "You're throwing you bloody life away you stupid little twerp. You wanna waste your life? Go get someone pregnant. It's better than getting yourself killed!" No chance of getting killed there though. Unless I was dying of thirst; or boredom. She'll be alright, I thought, once she sees how much stronger and better I am after being in the field. She'll soon change her mind. Or not; I don't suppose it really matters either way. But I did for once in my life, want to make the stupid cow proud of me.

I remember in school when I got sent home for punching this lad in the eye; she looked so disappointed in me. Like I was a piece of shit on her shoe. I always felt like I somehow had to make it up to her for that. Well, for all the times she gave me that look; just once I wanted to see her look at me the way she looked at my sister. She never even did much special, she got pregnant at fifteen. But now she got a supervisor role in the local Primark and I've never seen my mum look more proud in my life. Fuck, if that's all it takes, why can't she give that look to me? I don't know. Maybe I'm that bad.

Don't suppose she'd even noticed I was gone to be

honest. Don't suppose anyone had. It was just her and my sister back home. No girlfriend to speak of, and just a few mates dotted about. I did think of staying for this one girl, Dilly; beautiful she was, but bloody hell she wanted to move fast. Wanted me to move in after two months. I couldn't handle it. Not ready to play Mr & Mrs. I've seen that. Drove my Dad up the wall - no wonder he left.

I'd been sat on a crate of freeze-dried fucking carrots for about an hour. Top wrapped round my waist, letting the sweat drip down me as the sun browned me off like a bloody bourbon. All I can do is smoke to pass the time, I don't even like smoking, there's just bugger all else to do. Sit, smoke, think about what a stupid decision it was to come here.

Couple of the lads were playing a game of footie. But it's too hot if you ask me. Sam's always up for a game. He comes rocking into the tent like he's been snorting coke, looking wired as a fucking hyena, "Come on man, just a kick about. I need to burn my juices of. If I can't fuck at least I can pummel the ball". Lovely bloody image. I let him get on with it. He's roped in Dave and Tony, a couple of blokes with more muscle than brain. Could probably talk 'em into to just about anything if you had more than a few words in your vocabulary.

Last week I convinced 'em to nick some cigarettes

from the boys in the tent one over from us. Managed to nick a whole box of 'em. I stashed about twenty packets in my stuff before the lads cottoned on and had a big bust up. Nice to have some boys to do the dirty work for you.

Anyway, there they were kicking about their ball, soaking bloody wet from perspiration, panting like dogs and looking just as dumb. Then all of of a sudden Sam pelts the ball like a madman, sending it flying at full force into Tony's wet forehead. It slaps into him and sends silence like a bullet round the camp. Tony staggers a bit, looks a bit dumbfounded then collapses like a sack of rice, bam, straight into the floor sending a little clouds of dust sprinkling the air around him. I couldn't even be bothered to move. I was just fascinated by the whole spectacle of it. The sight of this tonne of bricks hitting the ground so hard, being taken down by the skinny little twerp. It was like David and Goliath, but less spectacular.

Sam fretted; running over to him like a concerned mother flapping his hands about. Dave was still taking the time to process what had happened, his thick skull moving as fast as an oil spill, getting stuck on reality.

Then, out he trots, lieutenant stick up his arse, Mason. Not much older than any of us, but he'd been bumped up the chain a bit faster cause he'd been to uni. Don't even know what he studied, probably fine art or some shit. But anyway, here he was somehow above the likes of a normal squaddie and taking every opportunity to flex a bit of power. He didn't know what he was doing with himself, the prat.

"Boys! Get a stretcher from the Med tent immediately! Man down!" He squawked at them.

"He's fine Sir, just a bash to the head from a football. He'll come round in a second." Sam fired back.

"I said get to the med tent. I've seen stuff like this before, an innocent bash to the head the next minute he's fitting and gushing blood from his eyes."

I don't know what Hollywood fluff he'd been watching to get that idea. But there was no arguing with the chain of command. Off Sam trotted like an obedient little puppy. He came back a few minutes late with a couple of lads in tow and a stretcher, just as promised. Skinny young things though, the lot of them. Don't know how they thought they'd get that lump up there. One of the lads I recognised. Young Welsh guy with a little too much tub around the middle and little too much to prove. The other lad though, Indian looking fella. Never seen him before, he somehow managed to keep some hair on his head, dark black. Wavy. He looked like he knew exactly what he was doing, like he'd seen more than half of these lads combined. Don't know where he'd come from. For some reason I couldn't stop myself from staring at him.

He knelt on the floor next to Tony and tried to roll him onto the stretcher, all three of them huffing and struggling like stuck pigs. Don't know how there was someone about the place I didn't know. Weren't many of us here. But then again, I suppose I don't take a lot of notice of most the men around here. Don't know why I noticed him so much. He just looked somehow out of place. Like he was that bit better than everyone else; and a little bit of him knew it.

They managed to get Tony onto the stretcher, and with some effort they carted him off to the medical tent for some well needed recuperation in the shade. I noticed a little tattoo on the medic's right wrist, couldn't quite make out what it was, but it almost looked like a little snake wriggling down his arm. And just like that, they were all gone. The whole yard was empty, except for particles of sand being blown about like shopping bags. Maybe I should have helped them, but I couldn't get my legs to move in that heat. It also felt like a small part of me didn't want to be seen by the medic. Like if he saw me, he'd be better than me too. He probably was, you needed some brains about you to be a medic here, most had come here from medical school but needed something a little bit more exciting than sitting in a GPs office.

I finally managed to get my feet moving and moved over to one of the empty guard towers surround the perimeter of the camp. Only a few of them were manned at the moment because the threat was so low. I climbed to the top and rested my arms against the relative cool of the metal bars. Looking out across that fucking dessert, I can't help but think there must be more to this than standing around. When am I gonna be able to prove myself? When am I actually going to make a difference?

I hope you enjoyed the book!

I'm an independent author so your feedback is really valuable. Please leave a review if you can or feel free to drop me some personal feedback to: tomnorthauthor@gmail.com If you would like to sign-up to my mailing list for offers and news on future releases please follow the link: https://mailchi.mp/1613c8979d1a/tom-north-narratotr

Thanks for reading!

Xx